E   508447
Hay   12.45
Hayes
This is the bear and the
     picnic lunch

DATE DUE			

For Helen with love
S.H.

For Christle, Mimi, Ruth and Didi
H.C.

Text copyright © 1988 by Sarah Hayes
Illustrations copyright © 1988 by Helen Craig

First U.S. edition

Library of Congress Catalog Card Number 88-81998
10 9 8 7 6 5 4 3 2 1

First published in 1988 in Great Britain by
Walker Books Ltd., London

Joy Street Books are published by
Little, Brown and Company (Inc).

Printed in Italy

THIS IS THE
BEAR
AND THE
PICNIC LUNCH

WRITTEN BY

Sarah Hayes

ILLUSTRATED BY

Helen Craig

Joy Street Books
Little Brown and Company
Boston · Toronto · London

This is the boy
who packed a lunch

of sandwiches, chips and
an apple to crunch

This is the bear
who guarded the box

while the boy went to find
his shoes and his socks.

This is the dog
who sneaked past the chair

toward the picnic lunch
and the brave guard bear.

This is the bear
with his eyes half closed
who did not notice
the dog's black nose.

This is the bear
who was sound asleep

when the dog took off with
a tremendous leap…

onto the table…

down to the floor…

and off to hide

behind the door...

and all that he left
of the picnic lunch
was an empty box and
an apple to crunch.

This is the boy

who looked everywhere

for his lunch and his dog
and his brave guard bear.

This is the boy
who heard the munch

of a dog and a bear
eating a lunch.

This is the boy
who tried to be angry

but decided instead

he was terribly hungry.

This is the boy
who packed a new lunch
of sandwiches, chips and
an apple to crunch.
And this is the bear who said,
"Haven't you guessed?
Picnics indoors are really
the best!"

F